# BONKERS!

Natasha Sharma

Illustrated by Deepti Sunder

Bullet, Kapoo, Zema, Ninjh, Chutki, Goofy, Buttons and Simba—for a childhood full of treasured memories. And for Obi Singh—the current and original Bonkers!

Big thank you, Payal Kapadia, for all your help.

Duckbill Books Pvt Ltd.
F2 Oyster Operaa, 35/36 Gangai Street Kalakshetra Colony,
Besant Nagar, Chennai 600090
www.duckbill.in
platypus@duckbill.in

First published by Duckbill Books


10 9 8 7 6 5

ISBN 978-93-83331-02-4

Typeset by Magic Touch

Printed at Sanat Printers, Kundli, Haryana

Also available as an ebook



Children's reading levels vary widely. The general reading levels are indicated by colour on the back cover. There are three levels: younger readers, middle readers and young adult readers. Within each level, the position of the dot indicates the reading complexity. Books for young adults may contain some slightly mature material.

# First Meeting

'I'm home ... WHAAAAT? WOW!'

My father is standing before me holding a wriggling, squirming, squealing mass of brown and white fur.

'Pant! Pant! Pant! Chuuueeeee! Chuueeeee!' squeals the fur ball.

I am sure it can't be ... but it is! Eyes wide, I drop down on my knees, as Papa puts down my long-awaited puppy. In a flash, the fur ball shoots forward and BAM! rams into my face. My spectacles go flying off my nose. I fumble for them.

Lick! Lick! Lick! Slobber! Slobber!

'Oh okay! Down, boy, down!' I laugh, my face wetter than a drippy washing line. Not-so-gentle nips and tugs on my hair now.

'Ow! What's that all about?' I wonder aloud, as I crawl around on all fours, squinting into space, in search of my spectacles.



'SQUEAL!'

I squish fur ball's tail under my hand. I reach out to pet him and feel something smooth and hard in his mouth. Aha!

'Give! Drop it! Good dog!' I say, smiling broadly at how intelligent my puppy is.

My smile disappears as fast as it

appeared when I see his blurry, furry behind running off, my spectacles still in his mouth. Two rounds of the living room, a close miss with the lamp, sounds of mother screaming, sister clapping, father grunting and me begging, and my brand-new pup's furry behind is now behind our gigantic furry sofa.

Gnawing, slurping sounds drift to my ears through the space below the couch. I cringe with every crunch. I clap

my hands, blow kisses his
way, snap my fingers, but
nothing works. The rest of
my family disappears, leaving
me to get back my spectacles myself.
Heartless.

Rushing to the biscuit jar, I come back armed with treats to tempt him out. I pick up the coffee table and huff and puff it out of my way. I roll the edge of the spiky carpet to give myself an extra inch of space. Then I lie down flat on my stomach and hold the biscuits out as far as my hand will go. The crunching stops for a moment. I sense a Sniff! Sniff! Sniff! And then the crunching starts again.

Who doesn't like Gluco biscuits, I wonder.

As I lie there munching, and puzzle over what to do next, little puffs of dust rise from the space where no one ever vacuums and …

AAAAHHHHCCCHHHHHHOOOOO!

AAHHCHOO!

AAHCHOO!

Startled by my machine-gun sneezes, a now-more-brown-than-white, startled fur ball rushes out squealing and drops a pair of mangled spectacles into my lap. Grabbing the little fellow with one hand, I pick up my glasses with the other. I wipe his saliva off my spectacles on the ugly sofa, and try and fix them back on my face. They've been bent out of shape, with little bite-marks on the frame, but at least the lenses aren't broken.

I hold up the pup and stare at him as his little behind goes into a wagging frenzy.

I have a dog!

'Hello,' I say. 'I'm Armaan.'

He responds with one big lick and a little nip on my nose—and I get the feeling that I have probably bitten off more than I can chew.

# How It All Began

Two life-changing things happened to me a few months ago.

The first was my biggest project of all time: Project Get a Dog. This, as you now know, I have been successful at. A dog has been on my wish list for three years. A few months ago I felt like the time had come for a final push. This is how I did it.

One: I pleaded.

'Any kind you like. Puh-leease. Small, big, medium, scruffy, lanky, furry, short coat, long ears, perky ears, wrap-into-a-bow ears, droopy eyes, pug nose, long nose, pointer, spaniel, retriever, terrier, hound … any kind! Any kind you like. Please, oh please, get me a dog! I promise to behave. I promise I'll do my homework. I promise I'll practise my keyboard. I promise I'll watch only one hour of TV a week. I promise I'll clean up after him. Pleeeeaaaase.'

Two: I wished and wished and wished.

I used every eyelash that fell on my cheek, and a few that belonged to my younger sister, to wish for a dog. I wished on shooting stars, on first stars in the sky, on the stars in the planetarium (even though I know those are fake).

I wished on birthday candles. I wished on full-moon nights, on Diwali, Christmas, New Year's Eve and even Holi. My cousin told me that wishing on a fart makes wishes come true. Even though I had a sneaky feeling that I was being tricked, I ate beans for a week. I really, really wanted a dog.

Three: I said clever things.

I searched newspapers, magazines and websites to help things along with my parents. Things like: 'Pets make children responsible', 'Dogs are the best protectors of your home', 'A dog today can keep the doctor away', 'Dogs keep your heart healthy'. (Okay, maybe I made the last two up, but dogs do make you happy so they probably keep you healthy.)

I love all animals, but when it came to a pet, it had to be a dog. A boy must have a cool, funny, brave sidekick and that's a role for a dog. In my case, I also REALLY need a protective dog by my side to save me from TT. Which brings me to the second life-changing thing.

I have been receiving needless attention from TT.

Who is TT? you ask.

I'll tell you this in a whisper (just in case he is around). TT is the wart on a witch's toe. He is the slime on a stinky sock, the gloop on a gooey gumball, the mush on a mangy mosquito ... I can go on. This big bully is three grades senior to me. He is the leader of the Ghastly Groundhog Gang, which is astonishing since he moved to our neighbourhood and to my school only six months ago.

The Groundhoggers are a bunch of boys who like nothing better than to pick a fight, push someone over or hog any place that they think should be theirs (which is anywhere they stand). No one knows TT's real name. I am certain it is horribly silly and that's why he keeps it a secret.

In any case, this is how it all began (or ended) for me.

I was walking down the school corridor on my way back from the library. My face was buried in my book, as the hero in the story was just about to jump off a cliff on a flying horse … when I walked headlong into TT.

Did I forget to say that I had my bottle of water open in one hand and a few generous swigs of water sloshing about in my mouth, too? In short, my book landed on TT's foot, the water from my bottle splashed on his clothes and as for the water in my mouth—I squirted that out on him when my mouth shot open in alarm.

Until then, I'd been careful not to attract the bully's attention. But at that moment, I got all of his attention. I soon lay flat on the ground, with TT sitting on top of me.

I am doomed till he forgets this frightful incident. My current master plan has been to stay out of TT's path as much as I can. It is a little difficult since he studies in my school and lives in my colony. I could do with a bodyguard.

You see why I need a dog?

And now I have one.

The little brown-and-white fur ball that made quite an entry yesterday is my very own dog. I look at him again through my crooked specs.

Protect me against TT?

Judging by his slurpy, nippy response to my first hello, I should say, 'Ha!'

Become my cool sidekick?

Let's see ... patchy fur, squat body, stumpy legs and panting-always-open mouth. 'Ha ha!'

If you were to move in closer for just a moment, I'd khuspus into your ear, 'I'm not so sure about my wish anymore.'

I know that's horrible. Don't look so shocked. It's just that it has been one day since the pup came home and I am in more trouble with the Groundhoggers

than I've ever been before.

Today, not only did TT push me in the bus and knock off my specs, he also noticed the bite-marks on the frames. Now he's telling everyone that I chew my specs when I'm nervous and that I have little white fangs that grow out at night to do this. Each time I cross him or his friends, they go, 'Woof woof! Where are your fangs now?'

My crooked glasses slide down my nose at will. I push them up with a trembling hand and take the longest route to my class, to avoid the Groundhoggers.

And about the dog. There is nothing to be done now. He's here and he's mine. And I'm down to one hour of TV a week.

Me and my big mouth.

# A Name

Every pet needs a name. I spend a few days getting to know my pup before thinking up a name that will suit him. He has spent a month nameless.

In the meantime, the little mutt responds to 'Dog', 'Oye', 'Pssst', 'Poochie Poochie Poochie', and 'AAAAAAAAAHHHHH!'

The last one is from Beeji, my

grandmother, who isn't the most dog-friendly person around. Each time the nameless mutt goes near her, my granny screams. The mutt now thinks that 'AAAAAAAAAHHHHH!' is also his name.

Also, I am quite fed up of trying to whistle to the pup. Especially since my younger sister Neha can do this really cool whistle, while I try with no luck at all. I usually sound like 'phuuussss', 'feeeee fee fee', 'phooo'.

With the dog responding to all these strange sounds, it is a state of emergency. I gather the family around the dining table and we begin.

'What will you eat, my baby? Meat curry? Kebabs? Come here now. Come to mama. So we need a name for you, coochie-coo? I gave both Armaan and Neha their names, so I should decide your name. We'll call you Poochie. What do you think, darling?' rattles my mother.

My father peers over his newspaper and says, 'Hmmm.'

'Poochie! So cute, Mama! How about Coochie-Poochie?' cries Neha.

'We can call him Poochie and his

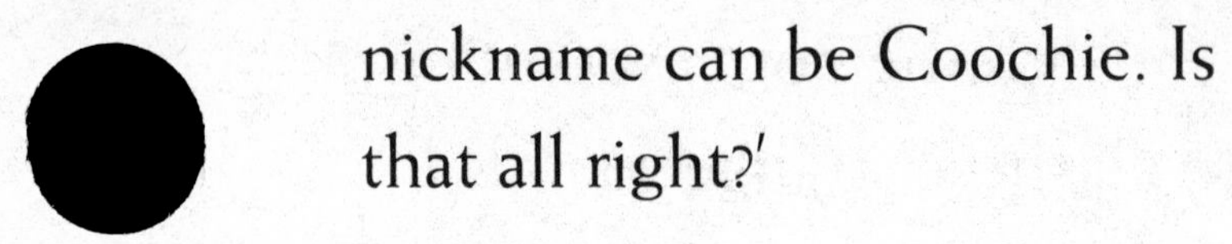

nickname can be Coochie. Is that all right?'

My sister nods her head up and down like one of her dolls.

'And what do you think, darling?' inquires my mother.

My father peers over his newspaper and says, 'Hmmm.'

I look on in disbelief, hoping that my friends, Guvi and Saumya, who are here for this all-important meeting, will say something. I can't take this Coochie-Poochie conversation anymore so I yell, 'Coochie? Poochie? No way! We are not calling him any of those names! Firstly, he is a male dog. And male dogs are not called Poochie! Secondly, what kind of a name is Poochie anyway?'

'Such stubbornness, Armaan! So much of this "no, no, no" for everything. Just try saying it aloud—Poochie Poochie Poochie,' my mother suggests.

'Or Oogie, Oogie–Woogie, Binky or Honey?' Neha chips in.

I hop from foot to foot, my hair flopping on my forehead. 'There is nothing in the world that is going to make me say that name. No Poochie! No Coochie Poochie! No Oogies, Woogies, Honeys, Bunnys or anything like that! Guvi, Saumya, say something!'

It is then that I notice my mother's clever plan. She has put a plate full of freshly-made laddoos in front of my loyal supporters. My mother's hand threatens to take the plate away even as Guvi stuffs his face with two more laddoos.

'Gurvinder Singh!' I exclaim in my seriously stern voice. It has no effect. 'Bubbbe Wubbe Mubbe,' he mumbles, with a curious shake of the head that leaves everyone trying to guess whose side he is on.

I am certain that Saumya will not let me down. 'Saum—' I turn to find her missing, laddoo plate and all.

'Well, Mama! This is a trick! Just to get your way! I am not going to let you!'

'That is no way to talk to your

mother,' says my father in a deep, low, terror-inducing voice reserved especially for occasions such as these.

I make my puppy-dog eyes at my father, hoping that he will jump in and fix this.

'Let the boy decide. It is his present after all,' announces Father. 'You owe me one. We're not going to get any dessert tonight,' he whispers in an aside.

I give him a wink and a nod. I'm quite certain that he is secretly pleased to have saved the family pet from a Coochie-Poochie fate. Mama and Neha settle back in their chairs with big grumps on their face because it's true—the dog is mine.

'Well, what is it, Mr Name-Genius? What are you going to call him?' asks Neha.

The mutt decides at this very moment to rush past with what looks like the remains of my ... my favourite rocket-powered, sleek, double-bounce, super-tread shoe!

'Flaming falooda!' mumbles Guvi. 'He's really in for it now.'

I yell out,

'STOP OAF!'

'SILLY FOOL!'

'YOU MUTT!'

'WHAT A ...!'

'What kind of names are these? Stopoof? Silifool? Yomutt? Whata? Have you lost your mind?' says my mother indignantly. I peel my eyes off the retreating behind of my dog, the shoe-sole hanging from the side of his mouth like a giant tongue, and stare at my mother in a daze.

The mutt, my long-awaited gift, then doubles back. Grinning wildly, he is extremely pleased with himself as he drops the chewed-on, saliva-soaked remains of my shoe at my feet. You would think he's obeyed a 'Fetch!' command!

I grab him, stare him in the eye and feel a thunderbolt as the name forms in my head—BONKERS!

'Bonkers,' I say in my firmest voice. 'We'll call him Bonkers.'

'Bonky Poochie it is then,' mutters my mother.

# Terrible Teething

Bonkers spends the next few weeks living up to his name and really getting into the role of a crazy dog. The ruining of my rocket-powered, sleek, double-bounce, super-tread shoe was just the beginning of an epic movie called *Bonkers Chews Up the House*.

His teeth seem to be in a wild hurry to sprout. Bonkers' gums are always

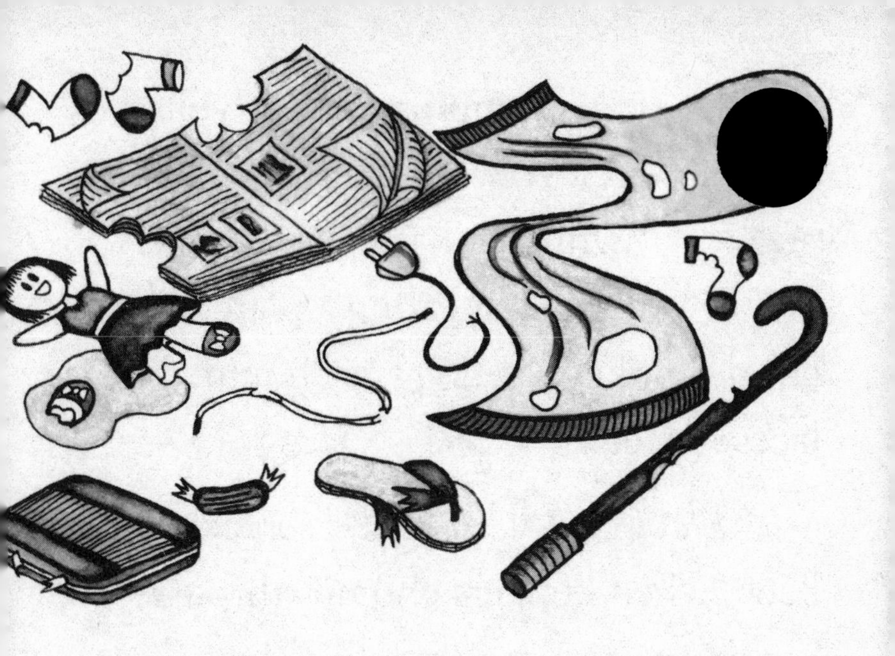

itchy and he needs to chew. It is chomp-gnaw-grind-munch accompanied by slobbery sounds all day. At the vet's suggestion I buy some dog toys and teething sticks, spending half this month's pocket money on them. They are sitting at the bottom of the drawer now as Bonkers makes his way through everything else in the house.

'Jumping jalebis!' yells Guvi, when he realises that while he has been merrily sitting and eating a plateful of chaat, Bonkers has chomped his laces for tea.

'AAAAAAAAAAHHHHHH!' screeches Beeji, when Bonkers chomps through her music-system wire while she is listening to her bhajans.

'That little monster,' mutters Papa, when he sees his morning paper shredded to bits before he has even read the headlines.

'AAAAAAAAAAHHHHHH!' screeches Beeji, when Bonkers chews up her chappals.

'Boo hoo hoo!' wails Neha, on seeing her doll short of one foot and a tiny doll sandal lying in a pool of spit. 'Armaan spoilt my doll, Mama.'

'What did I do? Why would I chew your doll's foot?' I gasp, as Bonkers zooms past me with that special speed he reaches right after a chew session.

'AAAAAAAAAAHHHHH!' screeches Beeji, when Bonkers munches up her walking stick.

'Here, here Bonky Poochie,' coos Mama, throwing down mutton bones for Bonkers to munch on, hoping that he will stop playing tug-of-war with her

already full-of-holes dupatta, and nearly strangling her.

'AAAAAAAAAAHHHHHH!'

Oh, well ... guess who?

'AAAAAAAAAAHHHHHH!' screeches Mama, this time, when the leg of her super-new dining table is chewed to splinters.

'AAAAAAAAAAHHHHHH!' thunders Papa, when his new super-padded laptop bag is suddenly without a handle.

'AAAAAAAAAAHHHHHH!' wails Neha, when her super-special stand-up-and-sing mike is now missing a wire.

Our home is full of chewed-up doorstoppers. Shredded socks litter our corridor. The pockmarked legs of our chairs match the chewed-up table. Frayed curtains hang from the windows. Most people have one slipper missing. I am now in everyone's bad books.

The strange thing is that it's me who is in trouble, and not Bonkers.

'He's just a pup.'

'You have to teach him, Armaan, and you are not doing a good job of it.'

'Control him.'

'Train him.'

And finally it is my turn.

'AAAAAAAAAAHHHHHH!' I yell, when I find my homework lying chewed up by my bedside before school. My teacher rolls her eyes when I tell her that my dog ate my homework. Why does it sound so unbelievable? If you have a dog like Bonkers at home, it would be strange if this did not happen. But my teacher does not seem to understand how crazy my dog can be.

'At least try to be original with your excuse, Armaan. For not doing your homework and such shoddy lying to top it, go stand in the corridor for the next hour. And don't move a muscle,' says my teacher.

Gulp.

Outside the safety of my classroom lies Ghastly Groundhog territory. My stomach churns with fear for I know what awaits me. TT is famous for working hard to be thrown out of class each day and he never stays where he is supposed to. This is his time to prowl the corridors and seek out prey. Today's prey, all thanks to Bonkers, is I.

I stand, not moving a muscle, eyes tightly shut, as I find myself being used as a target. For the next sixty minutes I peel spitballs off my face, shot at me through a straw by none other than the monstrous TT.

# TROUBLE. In Big Huge Capital Letters

Saumya read in a book that all babies, even dog babies, go through the two Ts. The first T is Teething and the second T is Toilet Training.

'That is three Ts,' I point out to her.

She blabbers on, 'So Armaan, you've just got to stop whining and keep up with it for a few more weeks. I think we

should take him to the colony park for a walk every evening and get him to pee and poo there.'

'Oh wonderful! I'll get done with mopping here and then go get mopped in the garden by the Groundhoggers,' I mutter.

There is no getting away from taking Bonkers for a walk though, now that he is a few months old. So we set out for our first visit to the neighbourhood park. It's a special moment and even though my dog is not as big, as handsome, as smart, as obedient, as … well … even though Bonkers isn't all I dreamt of in a dog, he is my dog.

It takes us twenty minutes to get to the park although it is a five-minute walk away. The first sign of trouble shows up when Bonkers walks, hops, twirls and swirls in the air, trying to catch the leash in his mouth and rip it apart.

Then he sits down in the middle of the road and tries to scratch the collar off his neck. When that doesn't work, he drags me to a nearby gate. Before I realise what he is planning, he sticks his head through the bars and starts to pull his neck back, hoping to leave the collar stuck there, while sliding his head out. I would normally be excited to see signs of such high intelligence in my

dog, but I quickly have to save him from ripping his head off.

I undo the collar to allow his head to come free. Bonkers lets out a yelp of joy and runs right back home, with me running and screaming behind him.

With the collar back on, we are on our way again, this time with the leash firmly between Bonkers' teeth.

We reach the ground. I carefully take us to the end farthest from where TT and his gang are playing cricket. TT is at the crease, looking ready to erupt, while yelling at the bowler and the umpire about the last ball being a no-ball.

'Come on, run around for a bit,' I

say to Bonkers; words I wish I had never said. As soon as I unhook the leash from his collar, he shoots past me like a bullet and runs in a straight line towards the cricket match. This is not good. Not good at all.

I chase Bonkers, my speed hampered by the loss of my rocket-powered, sleek, double-bounce, super-tread shoes. Straight ahead, I see TT pull his bat back, slice it through the air and whack the ball. The ball sails for what seems to be a boundary. The umpire has already begun to move his hand to signal four runs. That's when I see a flash as Bonkers jumps straight up before the boundary marker—and catches the ball in his mouth.

Uh oh!

He takes little chomps on the ball to satisfy his itchy gums, then turns around and makes a beeline for me.

Double uh oh!

Behind him charges the fiendish, fuming, frothing-at-the-mouth figure of TT, furious at having been got out by a catch, in addition to losing four runs.

Triple uh oh!

I somersault in the air and start

running in the opposite direction. Bonkers follows close at my heels, ball in mouth. I am impressed with my own running in this obstacle course. Maybe I'll try out for the obstacle race in sports day next year. I leap over a bush, trip over a kid, swerve to miss the ill-tempered aunty from House 182, do two skips in the middle of a skipping rope and then sprint twenty metres. But the dust we are kicking up in the garden has made its way up my nose and started off my sneeze attack again. What rotten luck!

That is when the large and heavy hand of TT clamps around my neck and brings me to a screeching stop. A sharp yelp from Bonkers means he's caught, too.

Like two puppets, we are turned around to face our tormentor!

'L-l-l-let us g-go please. We're s-s-sorry,' I blubber, my eyes streaming.

'Quiet!' thunders TT.

'Woof! Woof! Woof!' barks Bonkers.

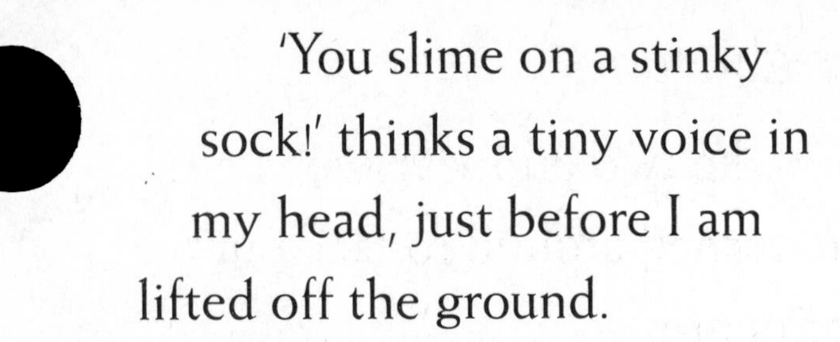

'You slime on a stinky sock!' thinks a tiny voice in my head, just before I am lifted off the ground.

Bonkers growls, twists and turns his body. He slips out of TT's grasp and drops to the ground. I look down, certain I will see him flee. Instead Bonkers stands, legs apart, two sparkling freshly sprouted teeth glinting in the sun.

'GRRRRRR! GRRRRR! GRRRRR!'

I suddenly feel much kinder towards my dog, even though he got me in this mess in the first place.

I look back at TT who seems to have

transformed into an awful ogre. His mouth is frothing. His hair stands up like sharp spears to stab me.

Through slitted eyes (I don't want the spit spewing out of his mouth to blind me) I see a huge hand drawing into a huge fist and getting ready to deliver a huge punch. That is when I feel the familiar twitching of nostril and itching of nose and ...



AHCHOOOOOO!

Oops! All over TT's face.

'Yaaah! Yuck!' he screams.

The shock and the spit make him drop me. I scoop up an alarmed Bonkers and start running. TT starts after us, and slips on a fresh pile of poop that Bonkers has deposited near his feet, just as I was about to be punched. I take one look backwards at TT, lying face down in the mud, and flee past open-mouthed Guvi and Saumya, who have just arrived at the park entrance.

# Dangerous Days

'I'm done for,' I moan to Guvi and Saumya.

Guvi has an upset tummy after hearing what happened on the ground. 'Bletchy broccoli!' he cries in alarm. 'You're done for! We are done for!'

'Thanks for reminding me,' I say, holding my head in my hands. 'Bonkers! What is wrong with you? Of all the

people, you had to catch TT's ball! I'm so gone.'

Bonkers looks up accusingly. He then flops his head down on his front paws and refuses to respond. I am pretty sure I hear him say, 'Well, you did tell me to run around and you sneezed all over him, too.'

'Enough, you two,' snaps Saumya. 'Bonkers is a dog and dogs like to run and catch balls.'

Bonkers' tail gives a happy wag.

'And he did stand by your side when that monster was threatening you. Armaan, the only thing you can do is stay close to me in school.'

'You'd better do that,' says Guvi, who

wouldn't be of much help seeing that he's always lost in his world of numbers and food. 'Everyone thinks twice before messing with Miss Karate Blue Belt here, including TT.'

Normally, I would not hang around any girl while in school, even Saumya, however great a friend she may be. But with no other option, I spend the next couple of days in her shadow. Thanks to Saumya's presence, TT has not completely flattened me into a chapati by now, but there have been many moments of terror.

The Groundhog Gang is in action.

A foot mysteriously appears and trips me over as I make my way to hand in my homework. The contents of my snack box are often on the floor. Even birds seem to be a part of the gang now for I have had five cases of bird droppings on my head in the last few days.

It's Friday, and the weekend is thankfully almost here. I walk into class after slinking around the girls during snack break. My school bag is lying on the teacher's desk—empty. My shoulders sag. 'Same prank twice in a week,' a silly voice in my head says. I am going to have to crawl around between the desks to find my stuff. I bend down and can't see a thing on the floor. Huh? I look around, biting my lip, and gape at the fan hanging from our super-high ceiling. The contents of my bag are dangling from the three fan-blades!

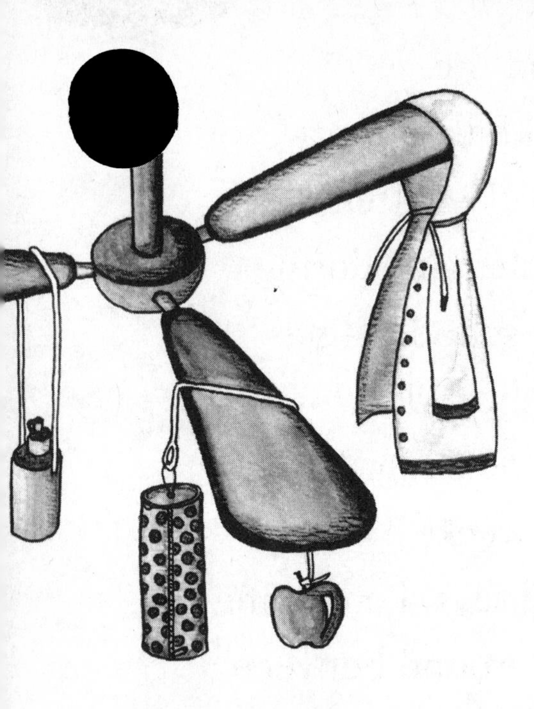

Some of the other kids come back in and they seem to see it as a challenge. A table is pushed forward, a wobbly chair is placed on top, a rickety stool goes on next and finally a stack of books is used to form a peak. One look at the unsteady mountain and I am chosen as the one for this mountaineering expedition. After all, it is my stuff.

I clamber onto the table. Gingerly, I step onto the chair. Then I creep onto the stool, blood pounding in my ears. I hate heights. Holding my breath, I somehow stand on tiptoe on the books. My legs feel like jelly. A dozen of my classmates are holding onto the various pieces of furniture that I am standing on and cheering me on. Beads of sweat trickle down my head. I look up and stretch

to reach my pencil case, when Guvi bursts into the room, munching on a greasy bread pakora.

'What's going on here?' he squawks. I almost jump out of my skin—not a good thing to do when you are standing on a towering pyramid.

Without losing a moment, Guvi goes CLICK on the fan switch, accompanied by a collective yell from the class. I am abandoned on my mountain as everyone ducks for cover. Things are flying off the fan like bullets. Guvi stands there frozen as I yell 'TURN IT OFF!' and somehow make it down in one piece (though I land with a thud, on my behind).

This has all the markings of Groundhogger meanness, though I have no way of proving it. I wish I could just stand there before TT and yell at him or something. I work up my courage, but I cannot say the words once I see him before me. If only Bonkers would grow up soon into a big, menacing dog and scare him away.



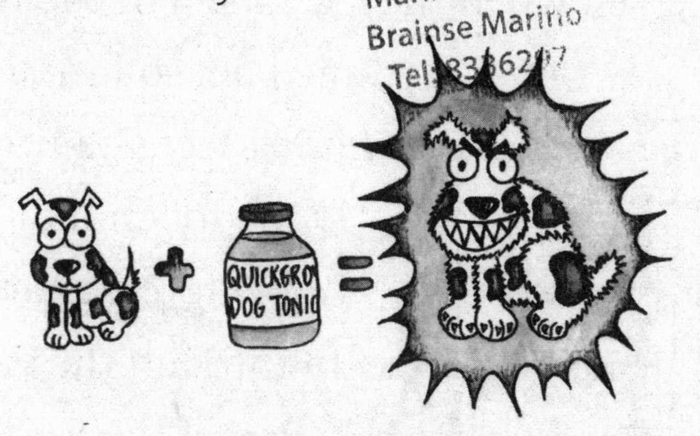


I have had enough for one day. Thankfully, school is out. I drag my smarting behind down my street, turn the corner, and look in horror! Five boys from the Groundhog Gang are standing outside my gate, poking sticks through the bars. Angry growls and yaps come from inside the gate. I start running.

'Is this squished-up excuse of an animal the one who caught our ball?' they yell when they see me. For the first time I am so furious, I don't feel afraid.

'Don't touch him!' I yell before dashing in through the gate. One of them tries to make a grab at me, when Mama pops her head out the door.

'What is happening here? Bonky! Armaan! Poochie! Are you all right?' (The names are now used interchangeably.)

The boys run off. I have never been so thankful for my mother's yell, even with the strange names. I go to my room shaking with anger and fear.

Every time TT crosses me in school he bends down and whispers in a sinister voice, 'I haven't forgotten, Spitface! I've thought of the perfect punishment. A water-dunking you won't forget.'

I want to remind him that he was the one left with spit on his face. Thankfully my mouth stays shut.

## Toilets and Trouble

Threats of a water dunking make it impossible for me to enter the school toilets. I am not taking a chance in the boys' restroom where Saumya cannot be around to protect me. By afternoon I'm hopping around, almost cross-legged, waiting for the school bell to ring and to rush home.

'TT's not going to forget about us, Bonkers! What are we going to do?

Please just stay out of his way. Okay?'

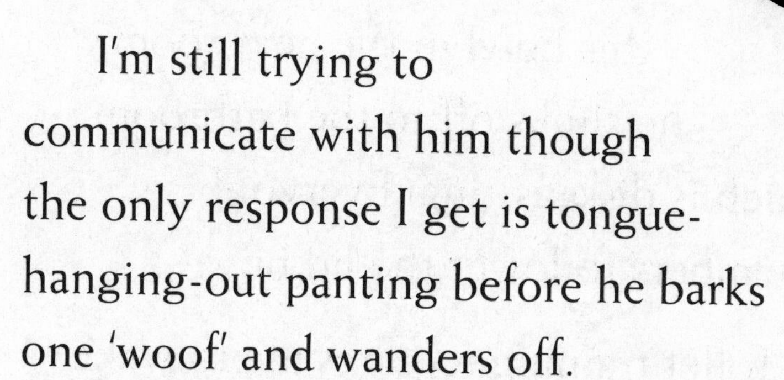

I'm still trying to communicate with him though the only response I get is tongue-hanging-out panting before he barks one 'woof' and wanders off.

With my mornings spent in terror of water-dunking, and the rest of the day spent toilet training Bonkers, I have liquid on my mind. I have realised that the amount of water this dog can drink can set a world record. He drinks buckets of it and I am always refilling the water bowl. When the

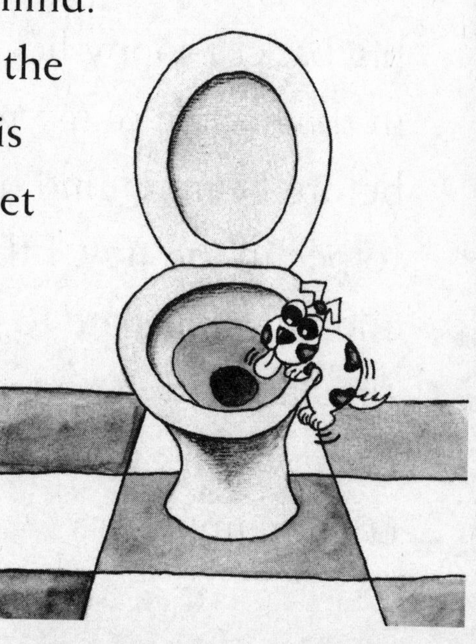

water runs out in his bowl
or he is too lazy to go to
his bowl in the next room,
he slinks off to the bathroom.
Which is dis-gus-ting! Everyone remembers to lower the lid now.

Toilet training requires me to wake up before Bonkers, grab him from his bed and make a dash for the pee-tray. But try as I might, Bonkers is always awake before me. He greets me with a big bark, a soppy lick and a giant puddle in the middle of my room. He squirts before I can remind him that he needs to pee in the tray. I think the barks and licks translate to, 'Rise and shine, Armaan, and get on with the mopping! I've got work to do. Few more puddles coming up!'

Slowly though, Bonkers understands where he needs to go when nature calls. I've avoided going to the park since I am on the radar of the Groundhog Gang, but I cannot put off taking Bonkers out for much longer. He needs his exercise. To avoid running into the Gang, I start going earlier in the evening, even though it is hot enough to fry an egg on the pavement!

Today, though it is still early, the big bully is already here. I'm really glad Guvi and Saumya are here, too. And I have to let Bonkers take a leak outdoors for he has been unusually thirsty and has drunk ten

bowls of water since morning. His stomach looks like a basketball. We stick to one scruffy corner as the Ghastly Groundhoggers have taken over the largest part of the park. Bonkers is happily running around between our legs, and we soon get busy playing hide-and-seek. It's my turn to find the others. I close my eyes and count down.

'10, 9, 8, 7, 6, 5, 4, 3, 2, 1 ... ready or not, here I come!'

Everyone is hiding, including Bonkers, and after two minutes of searching for the others without any luck, I yell, 'Bonkers! You are my partner. Don't hide. Come and help!'

'Boooonkerrrrs.'

'Bonkers.'

'Bonkers?'

'Bonkers? Bonkers? Bonkers???'

'Bonkers!!!!!!!!!!!!!!'

The last yell brings everyone jumping out into the open. We frantically search our area. I get a horrid feeling in my tummy as I look towards the other end of the ground. I groan and stare in horror, because Bonkers has reached the Groundhoggers' cricket game and is hovering close by.

'What is with this dog, cricket and TT?' I murmur in despair.

TT is wicket-keeping and is crouched down on his haunches waiting for the next ball. The team is watching the bowler and batsman. We are watching Bonkers and TT. And hopefully, god is watching over us.

Then in a streak of brown and white, Bonkers charges into the field. He reaches behind crouched-down-TT, lifts his leg and pees onto his crouched behind.

# Bonkers Takes Charge

I know my life is over, but my heart swells with pride, joy … and sheer terror. TT must have felt the wetness, for he feels his bum, smells his hand and straightens up, looking confused. He slowly turns around, just in time to see Bonkers fleeing the scene of crime.

Everyone is giggling and trying to hold their laughter for the fear they will be heard. TT stands for a few seconds, wondering what just happened. Then he charges behind Bonkers with a blood-curdling roar, 'I am going to squash you, you rat!'

This time it is Bonkers in the lead, TT behind him, Guvi, Saumya and I are third in the race, and the rest of the children stream behind us. We all run, puffing and panting, twice around the ground.

'That your dog, who messed with TT?' a kid asks.

'Yes,' I reply, as the kid gives me a thumbs-up.

'We need to think on our feet! How are we going to save that crazy dog and ourselves?' puffs Guvi.

'Bonkers! Where are you going?' yells Saumya as Bonkers suddenly changes track and heads in the direction of the community pool that is next to the park.

By the time I catch up, I am out of breath and ready to collapse. Bonkers and TT are already by the pool doing a catch-me-if-you-can dance. Bonkers is good at this since he has a lot of practice. TT steps to the left, circles, lunges and tries again as Bonkers weaves his way in and out of his reach. I get a strange feeling that Bonkers has a plan. He runs forming the figure of eight, as TT trips on his feet, flays his arms and goes SPLASH! into the pool, screaming.

It seems that I am not the only one tormented by TT. Everyone starts hooting.

Till we hear gasps and cries. 'Help! I can't swim! Help!'

I'm not a great swimmer, but I know enough to save someone. I jump in, swim across and grab TT who is so panicked that he starts pulling me down,

too. I cannot pull him by myself to the shallow end.

I hear another splash and see a furry head in the water swimming towards us, with a string in his mouth that is attached to a baby float. Bonkers paddles over with the colourful pink ring trailing behind him, flowers and butterflies printed on it. I grab at the float, squeeze it over TT's head and help his arms through.

We start swimming across the pool. I am in the lead. TT, in his pink-butterfly float, is holding onto my shoulders and floating along. Bonkers brings up the rear.

The other children are standing by the edge, cheering and clapping. I stand with Bonkers, enjoying our moment of glory. We are heroes, not just for saving TT, but also, I suspect, because we dared to take on a bully.

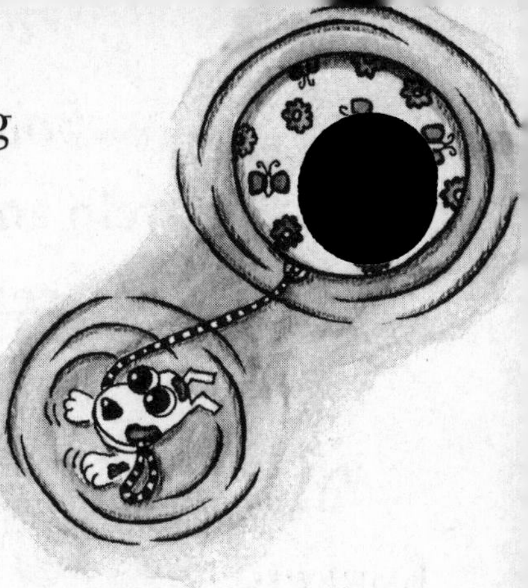

TT crawls out looking white in the face. I look at him and wonder how I was ever scared of him.

TT slowly stretches out his arm to shake hands with me. 'Thanks. I say we call it a truce,' he mumbles, staring at the floor. Then he lifts his head and looks towards Bonkers. 'But your dog ... he drives me insane. Keep him away. He's ... he's crazy,' TT whimpers before letting out a gigantic sneeze.

Bonkers gives a startled yelp and runs, tail tucked between legs. I grin and chase after him.

'Yes,' I shout back. 'He's positively Bonkers!'